THE
RAGGLESTONE
TODGER

A TALE OF GHOSTLY NAUGHTINESS

by
Royston Powell

Grosvenor House
Publishing Limited

The right of Royston Powell to be identified as the author of this
work has been asserted in accordance with Section 78
of the Copyright, Designs and Patents Act 1988

The book cover picture is copyright to Royston Powell

This book is published by
Grosvenor House Publishing Ltd
Link House
140 The Broadway, Tolworth, Surrey, KT6 7HT.
www.grosvenorhousepublishing.co.uk

A CIP record for this book
is available from the British Library

ISBN 978-1-78623-061-4

PROLOGUE

The tiny remote hamlet of Ragglestone consists of a few stone houses clustered around the only road into the village, which becomes a small dirt track leading to a large mansion hidden in the woods. It was a still, quiet night until the squealing of rats was heard and tearing down the main street came the vision of a naked, screaming Lord Prescot with a spectral rat hanging on to his unmentionable appendage. Behind him and his entourage of shadowlike rats, ran a half-naked maid hot in pursuit brandishing a meat cleaver.

Some of the villagers stirred, but turned over in their beds and went back to sleep; nothing new then.

CHAPTER ONE

The wind was blowing a northerly gale, and it was cold enough to worry brass monkeys, the rain was lashing down and the old house seemed to have a supernatural feel, but then the old house was always eerie. The battlements on the two end towers looked down on you like the mouth of an old hag mouth with several teeth missing and the gargoyles, which drained the water off the roof seemed to talk to you of times gone past when the old house was inhabited.

The house had once been owned by a Lord Prescot, who reputedly died of some plague or other; some say it was the Black Death. That was unlikely as it didn't reach the village, or as it was then just a few stone houses; no change there then, nobody ever came here, and nobody ever left.

It's said that Lord Prescot was bitten by a rat one night whilst he was in his cups, enjoying the company of one of the maids. His Lordship and the maid had been spreading cream on some interesting anatomical parts when he fell to the floor where a rat bit him on an unmentionable, but delicate part of his anatomy.

From what folks said at the time it was a wonder the rat didn't die of alcohol poisoning or something worse. Legend has it he ran out of the house and down the road to the village, hurtling down the main street absolutely starkers with one of the maids in hot pursuit wielding a meat cleaver. It must have been some sight to see, as it was rumoured that he still had the rat hanging on to his unmentionable for grim death.

It was a thought that brought tears to the eyes. It would account for the high-pitched scream that came from the house, and was sometimes heard in the village, where his ghost would occasionally run down the main street, if you could call it a main street; it was the only street. Lord Prescot had not been seen running through the village for a good few years now, the last time was during a snowstorm. That being the case it's a wonder his unmentionables didn't drop of, his feet must have been freezing, but his Lordship left no footprints.

The old house had been inhabited now and again over the years by the unwary, attracted to it by the fact that the price was very low, but nobody stayed very long, as the old house had a bad reputation. The present owner, who now lived in London, had left in a hurry, swearing never to return.

Not that this bothered Roger, to him the house's reputation was a good thing, and it kept the casual visitor away, which was handy with what he was up too. He was going to do some poaching, whatever the weather conditions, or the risks involved. Rodger was more afraid of the living than the dead, especial the bailiff who had the nastiest dog in the whole county, and was not averse to sending it after poachers. Not that the bailiff had any rights on this land, which had been abandoned by the absent owner.

Roger's backside could bear witness to the ferocity

of the bailiff's dog, but he had a family to feed and there was not much money about, so when poverty strikes you have to do the best you can. Tonight's poaching had been good, a couple of salmon and a good size hare. The hare was for the pot and the salmon to be exchanged at the village pub for his beer; well he did have to have some pleasure.

It was time to go, the swishing sound was due to start. This was the sound that kept even the bravest traveller away from the house on nights such as this, Roger was not afraid, but took no chances, and the warm fire and a pint at the Oak Inn was calling him.

He knew the swishing sound, he had heard it before, but the high-pitched, blood-curdling scream followed by the squealing of tortured rats was not to be hung around for. Some said that if you were too near the house when it happened your hair would turn white and you would never get a good night's sleep again.

Roger wasn't sure about that, but he was taking no chances, the pub was the best place to be on a night like this. The Oak was the only pub in the village, if you could call a few houses and a Post Office cum local shop a village; more a Hamlet than village. The shop charged the earth for things you could buy in a supermarket at half the price, but there was no bus service and not many could afford a car and anyway there were better things to spend money on. The beer at the Oak was first class, it came straight from the cask and sometimes if the brewery wagon didn't arrive the pub served the homebrew that Eric the landlord made, which was rumoured to be used to fuel Spitfires during the war! If it wasn't for the brewery wagon calling to deliver no one would know that Ragglestone existed, nestled on one of those wild remote moors that seemed to have been forgotten about by civilization. In the winter the village often got snowed in, but the locals were used to that, they could all perish and no one would know until the brewery wagon turned up.

Roger's home was nearer than the Oak, but the thought of that pint in front of the fire was more attractive than facing an irate wife who had not seen any money from him for about a month, if it was not for the garden and the chickens the family would have starved.

The Oak it was then, and well worth it when he considered the option of going home first and facing his wife stone cold sober, it was not a prospect worth thinking about.

"No contest," mumbled Roger, "the Oak it is."

The usual crew were in there, refugees from the storm, the kids and their wives. Wives who knew every other wife in the village and everything that went on, there were no secrets, the Gestapo had nothing on this lot. Roger thought they kept an account of how many beers were consumed, and where the money had come from. Eric swore that he never told anyone what went on in the pub, but then again he also had a wife!

Eric was the landlord and paid Roger for the salmon, not in cash but in kind, there was at least seven pints worth of salmon there. Not that anybody ever found out what happened to it, I don't think it was ever cooked in the Oak, some say he had a deal with the brewery for discount on the beer.

Roger repaid Burt the blacksmith the two pints he had bought him a few days ago when he was skint and was just settling down to his second pint when the door opened. Like one of those scenes from an old Wild West film everyone in the pub turned to the door in unison. There was a mortal fear that one of the wives would take it into her head to come down to the pub and drag someone home by his ear, or some other body part more painful, anybody else arriving was a stranger.

Panic was in everyone's eyes; it could have been a wife, or even worse still, the Squire looking for unpaid rent. But no, it was a stranger, well-dressed in an expensive raincoat and green wellies; a sure sign of a townie.

"Evening all, can I get you all a drink?"

There was a stampede to the bar' no one stood on ceremony when those immortal words were uttered; there was the chance that he might change his mind before you got there!

Everyone ordered a large whisky, but the newcomer didn't even blink when Eric told him how much it was, despite the fact he had suddenly increased the price up of whisky.

The well-dressed stranger with the townie wellies didn't bat an eyelid and when the rush to the bar subsided, he just looked around.

"My name is George, I have just bought the old house in the woods about a mile from here and this is the nearest pub, not only the nearest but the only one, so I thought I may as well make myself known to you all, seeing that I will be drinking here regularly and I hope you won't be offended by my offer to buy a round."

Not a word was uttered by the assembled mob at the bar until they turned as one to the bar, raised their glasses and said in unison: "THE TODGER."

The Oak's regulars didn't normally take to outsiders, but took to the newcomer immediately, they made an exception for rich people and idiots, and he must qualify on both counts if he had bought the old house. The newcomer was a good bloke for a townie; he bought the next round and settled down by the fire, when everyone moved over to make room for him.

The locals all introduced themselves, thinking if George was going to be regular for a few weeks they might as well make the most of his generosity as it would probably not last long. Not many who had bought the old house stayed for more than a few weeks. There had been a few town people who thought that country life would suit them, it may have done, but not in the old house. Some had tried to hold weekend parties, fat chance of that working out in this area. Neighbours for miles around avoided the village and the old house as if it were a leper colony; some of the owners had even left in the middle of the night, never to be seen again.

George looked around the bar. "I know you are all doing your best not to ask but I will tell you anyway, I am a Professor in paranormal activity at the University of London, I have heard that the old house has some unusual visitors, and I intend to find out if it is true. Some friends of mine bought it a few years ago, and have only recently recovered enough after a stay at a residential rest home for the bewildered to tell me about it. So here I am, and I intend to stay, I have taken a liking to the old place, bad vibes or no bad vibes.

"My daughters will be joining me shortly, they know about the house and its history. The surrounding area looks good for horse riding so they are looking forward to having horses again; their mother was a keen horsewoman. Sadly she was killed in a car accident some years ago, so I do tend to spoil my daughters."

Burt the blacksmith's eyes lit up, horses, shoeing, trade, money, beer; he was a farrier as well as a good blacksmith.

"I will need someone to bring the old stables up-to-date, anyone here who can do that?"

There was. George was going to be a most welcome addition to the village, especially his daughters; the local lads had been starved of talent for years, except for the occasional visiting females who had lost their way. The local girls were not even considered unless there were complications that required shotguns! All the local lads were told at a young age to look at the girl's mother as that will be what the daughter is like in years to come. That did tend to put the mockers on things. No females every came to Ragglestone unless they had a good reason, so of course the addition to the gene pool would be welcome, as nearly everyone was related in some way or another. This did produce the occasional idiot or genius and most of the village residents resembled each other, but the occasional idiot soon left the village and became an MP, or a solicitor, but they never came back, not even to visit. It is said that an idiot is a genius gone slightly wrong on the initial upward journey to the egg!

The evening went well, George bought a few more rounds and the locals felt they should return his generosity so Eric bought him a brandy. After all he had taken more over the bar that evening than he would normally take in a week. For Eric to buy a drink was noteworthy, apparently the last time it had happened was at the coronation celebrations, and nobody is really sure which coronation that was!

George wanted all the low down on the old house, no point hiding anything, he was told that there was a considerable amount of information in the squire's library up at The Grange, about three miles away and he would love to see someone who didn't owe him money. Half the village were in debt to the squire, most of them behind with their rents, but as he said, "better a little rent now and again than no rent at all, no point evicting any one. Who in his right mind would like to live in Ragglestone Village?"

George was warned that the squire had a very attractive daughter, who he had been trying to marry off to any likely man for years, so he needed to be on his guard.

George left the pub late with a few brandies under his belt, the walk back was pleasant now the rain had stopped and the wind had died down. The clouds had cleared and the moon was out, not a full moon yet, but there was enough light for him not to need a torch. Even if there had there been no moon the sky was so clear he could have made it home by star light, no light pollution, no street lights.

The old house did look eerie when seen by moonlight, it didn't bother George though, and this is what he was here for.

If rats were the problem, then some standard rat poison would do the trick, however how was he going to poison spectral rats? Not that he wanted too, he was here to confirm a theory not to act as an exorcist.

The odd thing about the house was that it did not have a name, it was just known as the old house, which really did fit so he was going to call it The Old House.

All was quiet as he opened the large oak door which was never locked, no one in his right mind would want to go in there anyway, that was according to the boys down the pub.

As George moved further into the house towards the kitchen he was met by a slight sound of swishing and squealing. It was coming from the kitchen and was to be expected according to the lads from the bar, now was his chance to confirm or debunk the stories that were rife in the village and what his friends who had lived here had told him.

As he approached the kitchen the sound grew louder, opening the door very slowly George peered through the crack, it creaked, the swishing and squealing sound stopped immediately. The moonlight streamed through the window and all was quiet, this is not what he wanted to see. George walked in and stood in the middle of the room.

"Lord Prescott, if you can hear me, your antics will not frighten me away from this house, in fact it will make me more likely to stay."

No response!

"I can wait," said George to the empty kitchen.

He was sure he heard a deep sigh.

A large scotch was in order before turning in, not that he hadn't had enough down at The Oak, but it was his custom to have a nightcap, and ghost or no ghost was going to change that.

CHAPTER TWO

The night passed quietly; mind you there would have to have been an earthquake to wake him after what he had put away down at the Oak. George had his breakfast in the kitchen, just toast and marmalade, he had not got around to hiring a cook cum housekeeper yet, and judging by what he heard in The Oak the previous night there was little chance of him getting one. On the other hand there must be some brave soul down in the village that needed some extra cash. It was not a live-in job so she could go home at night before the fun and games started.

The kitchen was just a normal kitchen during the day, the haunting only started at night, and then only on certain nights.

It was time for George to get back to the University and get his equipment, not that he really needed it, the place was haunted there was no doubt about that. The only fly in the ointment was how he was going to prove it to the satisfaction of the university grant board? However even if they didn't award him a grant he had enough money to continue without it, he had seen apparitions in the past and even taken photographs, but sadly they never came out. George knew what he saw but the camera did not record it for some reason. A photographer friend of Georges said that if the temperature fell too low the emulsion on the film would not be as effective as it should be.

One alternative would be to ask one of the grant board members down for the weekend, surely one of them would like a freebie weekend in the country? George considered this and was sure it could be arranged. One of the board members was in the same pony club as his daughters, so it would not be out of place to invite her down. On the other hand though, George didn't think she would accept on account that she had made amorous advances to him and he had been a little offhand with his response. According to his eldest daughter she was a bit of a dragon, she reckoned she modelled for the Welsh flag. He wondered if dragons could frighten away ghosts. On the other hand would a dragon take flight when confronted by a large ghostly bearded man swinging a broadsword?

The Grange where the squire lived was about three miles away, but it was a nice day so George decided to walk it, he doubted the Land Rover would have made it anyway as the area was mostly woodland with a few streams crisscrossing the estate.

"I have no idea where my land finishes and the squires begins," George said to himself as he jumped over another small stream. From his conversations with the regulars in the Oak the previous evening he learnt that his land was prime territory for poachers, not that he minded, at least it could be his contribution to the local community, even if it was illegal. George pondered on whether or not to give permission or just ignore it. "I will have to find out who the bailiff is and tell him not to bother anyone on my land," he decided.

The Squire's land ended about two miles from the Old House, so George's daughters would have plenty of riding without having to cross onto other peoples land. The villagers had gardens, but no land outside the village, there was some good fishing to be had, and there was quite few hares running around, so a shotgun licence was to be applied for as soon as possible.

"I wonder if I put silver pellets into the cartridge it would kill ghostly rats?" George said to himself, "It might be a last resort, but on the other hand would a cat with silver teeth be able to attack them?"

The squire's house was quite small in comparison to The Old House, the front door was open, but George knocked anyway. His knock was answered by a very attractive woman aged about forty, she had the kind of smile that put you at ease immediately and she had a figure that would have suited her for bikini modelling. Some lurid thoughts ran through George's mind, it was quite a while since he had any female companionship. Could this be the daughter that the lads in the pub say the squire wanted rid of? If so he thought he would be first in the queue.

"You must be the new owner of the old Prescot house, no one else ever bothers to knock, come on in. It's nice to see a new face; Dad is in the garden I will call him for you, in the meantime would you like a drink, scotch or brandy? That's all Dad ever keeps, although he has on occasion been known to drink tea or even coffee when he is desperate," she said with a smile.

"I expected a large manor house when they said they that we had a squire in the village." Said George.

She smiled, and shouted, "Dad we have a visitor."

George commented again that the size of the house was not what he would expect for a country squire.

"It's big enough for me and dad, and we don't entertain much, but now we have a new neighbour that might change. That is if you stay for a while, nobody else had stayed very long at Ragglestone House," she said.

"That must be the real name of the old house," George thought, not that he had seen any reference to it being called that anywhere, I know the village is called Ragglestone, so it would not be out of place for The Old House to be named after village, or the other way round.

A gruff voice was heard at the garden door, "make my day and tell me one of those reprobates from the village has come to pay some rent, I am running low on scotch."

The squire was a short stocky man, with a small neat beard, dressed in a pair of shorts and sandals and was not what his visitor had expected. "I don't know what I really expected," thought George, "perhaps a hacking jacket and tweeds."

He stopped in his tracks when he saw George and it was the very attractive woman who answered, "Dad this is George, he has bought the old Ragglestone property."

The squire reached out and shook his new neighbour's hand. "Glad to see the old place inhabited again, I hope you stay longer than the other townies that have moved in. Introductions, call me Jed, short for Jedediah, my Dad was very religious, this is my daughter Miriam, and on behalf of both of us welcome to Ragglestone. There is not much of it, but the folks who live there are very friendly and have been know on occasion to pay their rents. There is not much that goes on here, just the occasional hunt, which is just an excuse to go riding, we don't have dogs, I don't approve of that anyway, and we never catch anything, even when we do we let it go or there will be nothing to chase next year."

George took to him immediately, a straightforward local squire just as you would expect, except for the attire.

"I thought that I had better make myself known to you as I want a favour. Do you think I could read up on the history of The Old House, or as you know it Ragglestone? The lads in the pub last night told me that you had some records of it here, I am particularly interest in the Lord Prescot who died of rat bites."

"Well there are some records about in the library, but you would have to dig it out yourself, Miriam will give you a hand, she is always at a loose end except when she is out riding, which is quite often, do you ride George?"

He shook his head.

"Never mind," he said.

He directed George to a seat, "That's enough talking, has my daughter offered you a drink yet, if not I will. Brandy or scotch?"

He plumped for a scotch. The squire produced a bottle that looked to be a single malt with a cork and not a screw top; a sure sign of a good malt.

"Man after my own heart, I prefer our own homegrown spirits," said the squire. "I will only drink brandy when I run out of scotch, never did like the

French, they should be done for cruelty to frogs, what harm have frogs done to anybody? Tearing the legs of them, poor things can't hop about."

Things were not looking good; George could see common sense disappearing over the horizon with his arse on fire. Jed's daughter was standing behind him tapping her finger against her forehead.

"Is my daughter tapping her head behind my back? Jed asked George. "She does it to try to make out that I am not responsible for my actions. She thinks I am gaga. You by any chance single? I have been trying to get rid of her for years, nobody around here will have her because they would have to have me as well" he said with leery wink.

And with that Miriam turned on her heels and headed for the drinks cabinet, her rear view was really worth waiting for, it was like two ferrets fighting in a sack, and what a shapely sack. Poetry in motion was the only way to describe it.

The library was what George expected, floor to ceiling books all round the walls, many were very old and covered in dust, it was to a section like this that Miriam headed for, the books that she wanted were on the upper shelves so a sort of sliding ladder was brought round. As she was wearing a short skirt George hoped that she would climb the ladder, but no luck.

"You will have to fetch them yourself, I don't like ladders. Those are what you want," she said pointing to the upper shelves. "They go back centuries, long before the Lord Prescot that you are interested in. If there is anything you need just call."

The way she said that made George think that

anything meant anything and to be honest the way she emphasised the word *anything* did conjure up some erotic thoughts.

Back to the task in hand, when George climbed the ladder he found that rather than books there was a collection of parchments in old leather binders tied together with leather thongs. The records went back a very long way, nearly to Anglo Saxon times, Lord Prescot's ancestors had been part of the Norman Conquest.

The Prescot's were quite well liked by the locals, according to the records and there had at one time been a family church on the Prescot land, but it had been destroyed during the reign of Henry the eighth. The ruins were still there; George had noticed them when he surveyed the house before buying it and had a little wander around. He really enjoyed looking around old graveyards, there were a few headstones overgrown with moss and with the inscriptions quite illegible, worn away by the years, but some of the dates were still legible, and of course there were some recent ones. He had made a mental note to check and see if Lord Prescot was buried there.

He found a record of a grave giving the date of his death as thirteen forty something, which was about the end of the Black Death in England. The last figure was missing from the gravestone, but it did say thirteen forty something, so it could be Lord Prescot's final resting place. That is if he is resting or just in temporary quarters, one thing was sure he was still around as far as the old house and local legend was concerned. George wondered if they buried the rats with him.

Miriam came in a with two coffees, that made a nice change from the whisky that the squire had been pushing onto him, even if it was the finest whisky, Singleton single malt. She sat down opposite George, the front view was as good as the back view, he thought as he looked at her over his coffee cup; a very pleasant sight.

George was not really a breast man when it comes to the ladies, more of a leg man really, she had a fine pair of wobblers and he though that she couldn't have seen her shoes since puberty. And before he could stop himself he said, "Come over for a drink one evening, that is if you don't mind sharing the old house with my two daughters and of course Lord Prescot's ghost."

Miriam had a beautiful tinkling laugh, one which George could listen to all day; things were getting better and better. "I would love too, life here is very dull, and for some reason most of the local gentry try to avoid me, I think it's because of Dad and his drinking habits, I sometimes think that he is trying to get rid of me, but I also think he wants someone to move in who has money," she said with a big smile.

The walk back was to The Old House was pleasant, George saw quite a few rabbits and caught a glimpse of a deer. "If they were on my land," he thought, "could I legally shoot them? Not that I would, but on the other hand venison was quite nice." But killing a deer was like killing Bambi in George's book.

CHAPTER THREE

A couple of days later his two daughters arrived by taxi, the fare would have made any normal person's eyes water, but the girls never blinked. George realised it was a long way to come with no chance of a return fare for the driver before explaining to them about Lord Prescot. In return his daughters gave him a wry smile and a chorus of, "Yes dad," in a way that would humour the old man.

They then went off around the house at a gallop, every room was to be explored, the old furniture had been left by the previous owners when their father bought the house, not that you could move it out anyway, it must have been build in the house. They had decided where they were going to sleep and what rooms were to be theirs exclusively, their father told them that he was intent on proving or disproving the existence of the spectre of Lord Prescot. Not a problem, they were used to him searching for spooks and inwardly hoped that he would find one someday and if this were the place he would find what he was looking for then so be it.

Irene was the older of the two girls and said that she was looking forward to seeing Lord Prescot in the all together with a rat hanging off his interesting bits. She always was a bit of a tearaway. As far has her boy friend's were concerned, they did not seem last long, but she had gone to University and qualified as a doctor, not that she ever had any intention of putting it into practice, no pun intended, she did serve a year as an intern at a hospital, but that is as far as it went, she decided the hours were too long and there were too many drunks trying to take advantage of her, so that was the end of her medical career. George felt sorry for the local lads, if they thought that they were going to find some refined females, they were in for a shock.

Mary, the youngest of the two girls was a totally different character, her interest was of the equine nature; horses, she loved them, and would have spent all day on horseback and if she could fit a bed on one her family would hardly see her. When she did have the opportunity to go riding she took a flask and sandwiches with her and would not be seen all day.

So one of George's first tasks was to go to The Oak and enlist the aid of Burt the blacksmith and send him with his daughter Mary in search of local horses, there must be some stables in the vicinity, or maybe a local horse fair so Burt being a farrier would know where and his local knowledge would help to ensure she was not robbed, although Mary had a good knowledge of horses, so it would be a brave man who tried to catch her out.

Since their mothers death they had become very independent, George was always away following up on some report of a haunting somewhere, so they were left to fend for themselves quite a lot of the time. Often they would accompany their father when they were quite young and they really enjoyed themselves, children seem to like being frightened.

They soon got used to it, the only thing that frightened them now was a cut to their allowances. Fortunately their father's family were well off and his late wife's family were quite rich, so the girls had money put in trust for them until they were 25. Until then George was in charge of all funds, and he never curtailed their expenditure unless it was a punishment for something or other. So if they wanted to spend a fortune on horses they could do so, as long as they kept out of their father's hair.

The first thing Irene wanted to know was if there were any good looking boys about, George didn't want to disappoint her, as far as the village boys were concerned as he had never seen any of them. The clientele in The Oak were refugees from the marital home so he could not comment, but from what he gathered they were more interested in getting out of Ragglestone than anything else. "When my daughters get hold of them they will be scrambling over each other to get out even more than before," thought George.

It was getting near the time to introduce his wayward daughters to the locals and the only place to do this was in The Oak, no use putting it off any longer. They were champing at the bit to get to know the locals, especially Mary. She was keen to get to The Old House stables sorted out, they only needed minor work to get them usable, nothing major, and then she could go with Burt to the local horse fair.

The night the girls decided to go down to The Oak, was one of those nights when George would have preferred to stay at home by the fire with a good book and a glass of something nice, like a large relaxing glass of brandy. It was not to be, his daughters had made their minds up to go down to The Oak and that was that. There was no way their father was going to let them go on their own, not that he was worried about them, he was more concerned for the locals. Both girls could drink most people under the table and George knew that Mary would get Burt to do the jobs for next to nothing; good at business were his daughters.

The walk down to the pub was pleasant, the moon was full and millions of stars glittered in a pitch-black sky, with no street lamps in Ragglestone there was an unpolluted night sky, so no need for torches.

The only artificial light shone from The Oak's windows. The permanently lit fire in the bar sent smoke curling invitingly from the chimney. Some of the locals say the fire had never gone out in living memory, when the door opened the atmosphere was like a smog, the anti-smoking law hadn't reached this far yet, and when it did the locals would probably ignore it. This pleased the two girls as they had been smokers since they were at finishing school.

George didn't dare ask what they were smoking; there are some things a parent does not want to know. They were greeted with shout of, "what will you have." No doubt this would lead to George paying for the next six rounds or so. George had described Burt to Mary and she found him immediately, somehow George felt sorry for him and got the next round in. Burt and Mary were sitting by the blazing fire; it was like watching a Cobra mesmerizing its prey.

The door opened and gust of wind blew in causing the fire to flicker, as well as George's eyebrows, it was

Miriam, the Squire's daughter. The room fell silent, as she walked up to the bar and ordered a large gin and tonic, you could have cut the silence with a knife. It was reminiscent of a scene from a western movie when a gunslinger walked into the saloon.

Miriam smiled and looked around, "Calm down I'm not here to chase for rents."

That broke the spell; conversations resumed and if there had been a piano player he would have continued from where he left off. As she walked over to where Irene and George were sitting she smiled, it was like a burst of sunshine on a rainy day, George introduced her to Irene and the two girls looked at each other, you could tell that they had hit it off immediately.

Mary seldom stopped to see what was going on around her when the conversation was about horses, she was intent on getting Burt up to The Old House first thing in the morning and was busy discussing the current trends in horse riding gear and making plans to go riding as soon as possible.

Miriam must have had stables up at the Squires house, as she had ridden down to The Oak that night. Horseback seemed to be about the only mode of transport in Ragglestone after dark, certainly it was most of the time for those that could afford a horse, and if things were to get bad they would have no qualms about eating it. Nearly everyone else had bicycles, George had a Land Rover, which was essential as there were only dirt tracks out of the village, the tarmac road stopped at the end of the High Street, so his Land Rover was just an ornament since everywhere was a pleasant walk and there was nowhere to get fuel within a good ten mile radius of the village.

As soon as horse riding was mentioned Mary's ears pricked up and Burt became of secondary interest, she went over and joined Miriam's group, George didn't exist anymore so he joined the lads by the fire.

The conversation quickly turned to Lord Prescot and whether he had he made an appearance yet? If he had, did he have any clothes on and were George's daughters afraid of the apparition? George didn't dare tell them that they were looking forward to the sight, especially if he had no clothes on!

The rest of the evening went quite well, George's daughters kept the peace, which was a bit of a shock to him as after a few they tended to get a bit boisterous. The walk home was pleasant and it was then they dropped the bombshell, Miriam was coming over to dinner the following evening and their father suspected a bit of matchmaking was in progress here.

As they approached The Old Hall they noticed the front door was wide open; they hadn't locked it when they went out earlier, but they hadn't left it open either. No point locking it, when the locals would not come anywhere near it for love nor money; it was then they heard the squealing and the swishing, Lord Prescot must be active.

The girls very nearly broke into a run to get to the house first, they stopped dead in their tracks when the apparition of Lord Prescot materialised in front of them. He was a big man with a jet-black beard and a scar than ran from his eye to his chin and he had a rat hanging of his dangly bit. He let out a mighty roar, waved his sword and ran off towards the village accompanied by a retinue of about ten rats and what looked like a kitchen maid in hot pursuit wielding a cleaver. The two them and a few rats passed right through George; it was like a cold wind, the chill went right through to his bones, the girls just stood there.

They turned to their father as one and said; "if every we doubted your theories we are truly sorry."

At last, no more jibes about his research. When they got into the house they settled down to decide where they should go from there. George half suspected that the girls would not want to stay in a haunted manor! Wrong! They were keener now that there was some excitement to be had, they wanted to set a trap to try and catch some of the rats to see if they were real or not.

George told them this was a stupid idea, and more to the point what were they going to use for bait?

It was Mary that spoke up. "We can always ask Miriam to come over and bring some cream."

This of course brought a peal of laughter from Irene, and a scowl from their father, his daughters could be a bit crude at times.

"I suppose that you didn't notice that Prescot and the maid ran through you but some of the rats went round you?" Mary observed.

That meant only one thing, they were real rats, George had not noticed if there were any rats in the house before, well it was time to do a good study of the Manor and get a cat, a big cat, a bloody big cat, the rats that were pursuing Prescot were about the size of Yorkshire terriers.

George didn't fancy them running around the

house, even if they were not to be seen, they were still there somewhere, or did they only haunt Lord Prescot? By all accounts he was not such a bad Lord of the Manor, a bit over friendly with the women folk, they reckon that most of the population hereabouts are related to him in one way or another.

"That is probably why the village had so many geniuses and idiots from inbreeding," George thought. "What I would really like to do was do a DNA test on the villagers and find out how many of them are related to the old Lord Prescot."

George pondered on where he could get a DNA sample of him, certainly not from a ghost. He could dig him up and get one from his corpse, but he didn't think he would get permission to dig him up, not that there would be much left after all this time, but knowing the villagers one of them would probably do it for the right amount. A vision went through his mind of a moonless night with a couple of dark shapes digging up some old bones, and arguing as to which bone to take. It really didn't bear thinking about, but as things transpired there was no need.

The next day Miriam came round with a spare horse in tow for Mary. The two of them seemed to have hit it off, which was a good thing really, as meant that George could now devote his time to researching the manifestation of Lord Prescot and his entourage of ghostly rats. He had heard of ghostly horses but not rats and supposed that there must have been one or two sometime in the past.

As Miriam was here at The Old Hall George thought it would be a good idea to go over to see the old squire, at least he wouldn't be trying to get him to take Miriam of his hands, that was if he was sober enough to talk, which according to the locals would be quite new experience for him.

He decided to walk over, thinking the exercise would do him good, as it happens it was a good idea, as he met Roger on the way and he decided to walk some way with George, not all the way as the old squire might grab him for his rent if he came too near.

"We seen the old Lord Prescot do his streak last night, what did you do to disturb him it's not his usual time?" Roger asked.

"I didn't realise that there were certain time for him to appear," replied George.

"Normally he only appears when there is a new moon, but some of us think that if there are outside females in the house this would trigger his appearance, and you have two attractive daughters, both to put I mildly would put a stalk on a statue, if you will pardon the expression," said Roger.

This gave George food for thought, if the villagers were his descendants, local females would not be of interest to him, what was rather puzzling was where does he go and what does he do?

"Where does he go to or does he come back to The Old House? The night we saw him he did not come back, has anybody ever bothered to find out?" George asked.

He shrugged, gave George a wink and said. "Can't stop now, getting too near the squires and I owe at least six month's rent, call down to The Oak tonight and we can talk freely," he said folding his poachers gun in half and hiding it in a deep pocket inside his coat.

The Grange door was wide open as before, it seems no one locks things around here, apparently they have nothing worth stealing, or they know that if anything went missing it would be found around Ragglestone somewhere.

I went through to the garden, as there did not seem to be anyone around the house, and sure enough there he was stretched on a lounger with a glass in his hand; he never turned around.

"Come and join me in a glass of this fine whisky," he said waving the glass at George.

"How did you know who it was?" George asked.

"Nobody else around here comes to visit me, certainly not the villagers, they owe too much rent. They do pay now and again when they have had a good day on the horses, Burt the blacksmith gets some good tips from some of the stables he shoes for, and to give them their due they do pay up when they win. Too what do I owe the honour of your company this afternoon? If you have come to see Miriam she has gone off horse riding," he said waving a whisky glass in the air.

"Sure I can't tempt you George?" he said.

The way he drinks I should think that his liver is about ready for the pickle jar, and that is without the vinegar, thought George. "I need some information about Lord Prescot's ghost," he said more in hope that expectation.

"I can't help you much there, the only thing I know that is he sometimes runs through the village with a rat hanging of his dangler," replied the squire.

Dangler, it must a local term for what is called all sorts of thing around the country, chopper, old boy, willy, John Thomas, the meat injection, the mutton dagger the one eyed trouser viper and many other names to crude to mention, not that knowing that helped in any way, George decided that a glass of whisky would go down well all of a sudden, if it was loosening up the squires memory.

The squire's family had lived here for about two generations, so there was no way they could be genetically related to any of the villagers. It would be no good taking a DNA sample from him, anyway it would only give an alcohol reading far in excess of one preventing him from driving a vehicle.

Anyway the whisky was good, the weather was fine, why not spend a little time with the old squire, "you never know what gems of information might come up," thought George.

As it happened it was a pleasant afternoon and George needed to wind down before I went up to the University. He needed to collect scientific instruments that were essential to gain the proof that he needed to justify his budget for next year; not that the budget was essential, he could continue without it, and would do so if necessary.

CHAPTER FOUR

George quite enjoyed living in the countryside, especially in Ragglestone, the place had a character all of its own, which had long disappeared from much of rural England and Ragglestone really was rural England at its best. The girls, for the first time in many years since their mother had died, were making plans, something they had never done before, they had followed their father from one university city to another and they never really settled. George saw Ragglestone as his chance to settle down himself, there was enough going on at The Old House to keep him occupied for years. If he could prove scientifically that there was an afterlife never mind proving how bizarre it was, he would have done mankind a service by proving that there was an existence beyond this one.

The walk home was pleasant, no deer to be seen this time, "I will have to ask the squire next time if they are his or mine," George thought to himself.

He got up early to go up to the university to collect the equipment to prove that there was a presence in The Old House and justify his grant for the next year. Breakfast was the usual, toast and marmite.

"I will have to get a cook cum housekeeper," he thought, "this is one job I cannot leave to my daughters or I will end up with Miriam, you can bet on that, no, it had to be someone from the village, or failing that I will have to advertise on one of the University noticeboard and god alone knows what I will get."

He managed to get to a petrol station on just fumes with his Range Rover, it's no wonder there are no cars in Raggleston you could run out of petrol just getting to fill up. George decided to get some jerry cans to take back, the drive to the university was a pleasure, and he had called ahead for his assistant to meet him at the local pub where he could book in for the night.

Helen was a first class assistant, a bit on the young side and very attractive, but that was good, an unpolluted mind was just what he needed for his research and she was a believer in his studies. It had been weeks since George had been to his lab so what she had been up to in the meantime he had no idea.

The two meet at the pub for diner so that Helen could update George on how things were progressing with the information that he had sent her about The Old House and Lord Prescot.

The Plough was a nice quiet pub where most of the visiting dignitaries to the University stayed when they had a lecture to deliver, there were not many in tonight so a quite meal was envisaged, but as things transpired it was not to be.

Helen arrived with a young man in tow. "Professor, this is Lee from the science department, he thinks that he has a new camera that will take pictures of any spectral phenomenon, whatever the circumstances, even if they are not visible to the naked eye," she said.

This was good news, in the past the camera work just did not show up what the naked eye could see.

So, George had no gripe about buying a meal for the three of them, if what Helen said was true and Lee could deliver. But would he be happy to spend some time in Ragglestone? From what he had heard in The Oak the local girls were always on the lookout for new blood, let alone his two daughters who were always on the lookout for 'fresh meat', as they so delicately put it. They could be quite predatory when it came to men.

It was then that Lee produced his camera and started to explain how it worked. I was never one to take much notice of gadgets, but he pointed it at me and said, "It's simple, just point and shoot, the image appears immediately on the back and you then plug it into your computer and print it out." The camera clicked, which was unusual as digital cameras are usually silent, but Lee had adapted it to sound like a traditional camera, which according to him sounded more natural.

He smiled and looked at the image, which instantly appeared on the back of this state-of-the-art camera, the smile did not last, he showed it to Helen, not a word was said as he turned the camera around and showed George the image. He nearly collapsed; standing next to him in the photo was Lord Prescot with a number of rats scuttling around his feet. George must have retained his image when Lord Prescot ran through him.

That of course put an end to the evening meal, they didn't feel like anything to eat, but a few drinks were in order and as far as the apparitions were concerned they didn't bother George, but they did bother Helen and Lee.

"Well! What are they doing'?" George asked.

Lee changed to camera to video mode. "The rats are just sitting there looking at us and the big man with the black beard is just looking around. Oh! He has a rat dangling from his you know what."

That brought the evening to an end, if George was to be haunted he thought he may as well make the most of it, he had been trying for years to prove the existence and now he had the absolute proof, but not in the way he would have liked. George asked Lee if he could hang on to the camera, not that it would do much good. How could he take a picture of himself and the apparition, which was needed to prove that they existed, he could try a mirror he thought, but were they like vampires and cast no reflection?

"No chance of that, it cost a fortune to develop and the University would not allow it out of my possession," lee replied.

It was Helen who chimed in, "We could come down and stay for a while, that is if you don't mind and you have the room."

"Of course you can, you will have to ring me on my mobile when you are ready, there are no land lines in Ragglestone, and I warn you it is a bit out in the wilds. You don't by any chance have a mobile phone number that that I can call you on?" George asked Lee, who gave him a card that had his mobile number on.

This all became academic, as when they were making their way out of the restaurant a lady approached them. She must have been in her fifties, a bit on the plump side, but neatly dressed. George could never tell how old people were these days; people seemed to be much younger than they first appeared.

"I hope you don't mind me approaching you, but I am a very well known medium and you are being followed by a group who don't seem to want to be with you. They do look a comical lot, especially the one with a rat dangling from a certain part of his anatomy," she said with a smile.

"You can see them?" George asked.

"Yes and I can hear them as well, the rats are squeaking, the man is mumbling to himself about something that he wants back and there seems to be very faint image of a young female behind him with some sort of kitchen implement in her hand, they are going to follow you until he gets back what he wants."

"Many people say that these people are cranks," though George, "but now I can vouch for them," what with the absolute proof that Lee has with his camera. George wondered how he could convince the sceptics who will say it's a con trick and the image has been created by the clever technology that digital cameras contain.

The lady introduced herself as Maude and asked if she could get in touch with us again.

"If she can hear Lord Prescot I certainly want her to get in touch," thought George as he gave her his mobile number and asked her to call at the University tomorrow so they could have a long chat about Lord Prescot. Things were looking up.

The University buildings were very modern with lots of reflective glass and a huge foyer where a receptionist sat. She was the sort of person that would turn the Queen away if she was not wearing a Crown and carrying the correct ID. Not that it would have been a problem for the Queen, all she would have to do was produce a coin, but then of course royalty don't carry money. George had not brought his ID with him, so he had to get Helen to come down and vouch for him, which of course spoke volumes about his attendance at the department.

His department was on the top floor, in an area that was usually reserved for the idiot departments. Departments that were tolerated but not accepted by the University, but the grants came in handy. George always thought he got his Professorship by virtue of the fact no other idiot wanted it.

When they got to the department Maud was there waiting.

"Good to see you Maude, you are a bit early," he said.

"I am not going to let a chance like this go begging, I have been waiting years for something as good as this, and when I saw them all in the restaurant there was no way I was going to let you go, I was afraid you might think I was some sort of crank, but when I saw your reaction to the picture it gave me the courage to approach you. So what do you want me to do? I am retired and have all the time in the world and it's at your disposal," she said with a smile a mile wide.

George thought that Maude would fit in with the project perfectly in fact he would have pleaded with her to join them.

"Are they still with us " he asked.

"Yes, but there is only him, but the dangly bit and rats have gone and he is slowly becoming transparent, so he must be going back to wherever he came from, I take it you know where that is."

George explained about Ragglestone, the old house and the story that went with Lord Prescot.

"Will it be possible for me to come and stay for a few days, I won't get in your way, I will be as quiet as a mouse, or in this case a spectral rat and I am quite a good cook." She said.

Things were working out perfectly, George needed a cook anyway, his daughters could only cook the top class cuisine that they were taught at finishing school and he liked plain food. He told Maude that it would be fine and it saved him asking her, she was so excited he thought for a minute she was going to do a dance.

Lee arrived with all his expensive looking equipment. If it does the job and the powers that be argue about the cost I will personally reimburse the University, thought George.

Lee had a huge grin spreading across his face. "I printed out the pictures and they are unbelievable, the detail is a bit fuzzy but you can clearly see them," he said.

They were good, they showed George sitting at the table and Lord Prescot was standing behind him, he was just as I saw him back at The Old House and the rats were as clear as crystal. More so than the old Lord himself who looked quite bewildered, not surprising really as he could see everyone. That was one aspect that George though he would really look into a bit more deeply, if for some reason we could communicate with the ghosts, history would benefit to a tremendous extent.

There were uses for this camera that made George's mind boggle, could it be adjusted to take verbal communications or lip read? Could you just set it up in somewhere like the Tower of London and question the ghost of Ann Boleyn? What would you talk to, the head or the body, and were they back together?

All this was academic at the moment as George had Lord Prescot to sort out. Lord Prescot had the uneasy feeling of a middle aged woman by the name of Maude watching him all the time, as if he was some sort of exhibition, well really he was to her.

We sorted out the permission to take the camera to Ragglestone with the powers that be at the University. They were not very happy to see it leave the vicinity of the University, so I told them that I would pay for it should there be any problems. That settled it, so I had to sign for the camera, and after all that we decided to head back to Ragglestone the next day.

George offered to take Maude back home, she gave him directions and they ended up in Knightsbridge, outside a large house.

"Do you live alone in this big house" George asked.

"Yes just me and my cat Patch, but I have a housekeeper who lives in when I am away, so there will be no problem if I can't take Patch with me. As I told you he is quite a large cat and does not go out, so he has a lot of house to roam around in and an enclosed garden, so he is not restricted, and before you ask my father left me the house and a very large amount of money,"

"He was some sort of banker in the city and made a fortune in oil. My mother died giving birth to me so I was an only child, and was spoilt rotten."

A young woman who must have been the housekeeper greeted us at the front door. The house was what you might expect of a spinster who lives on her own in a house that has not been changed since it was build in Victorian times, oak panelling and a wide staircase ran up from the middle of the hall which was big enough to double as a ballroom.

We were greeted by Patch, Maude was right he was not just big, in the dark he could have passed for a medium sized Panther.

"Maude I would be quite happy for you to bring Patch down to Ragglestone, he might be able to catch some of the real rats that seem to inhabit The Old House, and you never know he may be able to see the spectral variety," offered George.

This brought a big smile from Maude. "I was sort of hoping that you might like the idea when you seen Patch, as far as spectral rats are concerned you never know, cats can sense and see things that are beyond us. He is quite friendly with people, but he does like to climb into bed with people when they visit, not that I have many visitors, people seem to think I am some sort of crank."

"On cold nights down in Ragglestone Patch would be quite welcome to cuddle up in my bed, that's if there was room, my daughters seem to be hell bend on getting Miriam into it," thought George. "I don't think I would mind all that much, but it may cause complications, which I could do without at the moment, and god knows what reaction there would be in the village, I would be the butt of all jokes for years to come."

CHAPTER FIVE

As we drove through the village of Ragglestone and approached The Old House Maude looked at me and said, "This place is alive with the vibes of people who have past on and have not departed, the whole village seem to be inter-related with Lord Prescot, I could spend a lifetime here and not scratch the surface. There seems to be something here which ties the whole village to Lord Prescot and him to them."

That was not difficult to work out! The drive back to Ragglestone had been much more pleasant than the drive up, George had Maud and Patch for company. Patch was loose in the car, but he just sat and watched the countryside.

Maud was apparently a well-respected medium in the spiritualist church and gave lectures at many of their conventions all over the world. George had always considered spiritualists to be cranks. In the past Maude would have been burned at the stake, not anymore, and his research would give her credibility with the non believers in the general public, that is of course if he could prove to the University Faculty that his research was valid.

The Old House came into view and George could see there were men everywhere, renovating the stables and refurbishing the outbuildings. Burt the blacksmith and his two sons were busy at what had been the old forge and overseeing the whole crowd was Mary.

There was no sign of Irene and when George asked Mary where she was he got a very evasive reply about something that had happened in the Oak last night and he should talk to Roger about it. The only problem was there was no sign of Roger and right now George had no desire to go looking for him.

As George and his guests walked through the front door Maud stopped in her tracks and went very quiet. "This house is full of vibes from many centuries of Prescots, and they all want to leave."

Patch stopped dead in his tracks and his fur stood up on end. Maud just stroked him and said, "Yes Patch I can see them as well, but don't let them bother you we can get rid of them later".

"Hold on Maude I don't want to get rid of them just yet, I have my theories to confirm to the University before we do anything like getting rid of any one of them," said George.

Maude gave him a big smile and gave Patch a pat of the head, his fur settled down and he gave a loud meow. "There are a few here who don't want to stay and some who do want to stay and pass on some messages. This might just be a theory for you to prove, but for me this place is like an internet hub, there are spirits here from all over, I am going to have whale of time, I want you to find me the oldest map of the area that you can," she said.

"That won't be problem, the squire up at The Grange has some very old maps. I saw them when I was researching this house, I will take you up there later," replied George. "I don't know what you would expect a Squire to look like, but prepare yourself for a shock. Right now I have to find out what happened at The Oak last night and where my daughter Irene is and make sure she is not causing any problems."

More in hope that expectations, there was a polite cough behind George and Maude, it was Miriam.

"Sorry to interrupt George, but I think that you had better go down to Roger's cottage, there is nothing wrong but Irene would like you to call down as soon as you are back."

Maude chipped in. "Don't mind me, I can look after myself and I really would like to have a wander around the house on my own. Well not quite on my own, Patch will be with me. I don't want him wandering off on his own yet until he gets used the place. I need to find the room with the most vibes and that will be the room that I want."

George didn't mind, there were ten bedrooms upstairs and god knows how many reception rooms on the ground floor, including a snooker room, the table needed to be re-clothed and that was something he needed to see too. He liked a game of snooker as did the two girls, and they were not too bad at it as some of the young bloods on the pool table down at the local pubs had found out to their cost. The girls seemed to be settling down quite well. Well Mary was, horses were her life and George could foresee her settling down here, but he had his doubts about Irene, and thought he had better go down to Rogers cottage and find out what had occurred last night.

George decided to walk down; it would be easier to leave Maude to unload her luggage from the car herself. There was a slight snag about going to Roger's cottage; he had no idea where it was! The only way to find out was to call in at The Oak, and that was a diversion he had no complaints about. A pint to steady his nerves before he went to Rogers's cottage, heaven alone knows what Irene had been up too.

George was greeted by a smiling Eric.

"I am not stopping for long Eric, I just want directions to Roger's cottage," said George.

"No need, he is in the bar," Eric replied.

The sight that greeted George was Roger and Irene sitting by the fire with a glass of brandy each.

"Come and join us," he said.

I gave them my sternest look, which I usually kept for students when they were larking about in class.

"Irene you know I don't approve of drinking in the day, if you have an excuse it had better be a good one," George said to his daughter.

Roger stood up, "We are wetting the baby's head, my wife gave birth to twins last night with the able assistance of your daughter, I have just learned that she is a fully qualified doctor. There was no time to get the midwife and she did the job expertly."

Irene just gave her dad a big smile. "You have to join us for one at least, just to be sociable," she said.

"I was under the impression that you no longer wished to practice medicine and just stay a plain Miss and drop the Dr," George replied.

"What I said was I no longer wished to practice in a hospital, General Practice is totally different and last night was an emergency. In fact if we intend to stay in Ragglestone I may open a surgery and go into General Practice, heaven knows the nearest Doctors is at least ten miles away," she said.

The idea of Irene as a GP was something George had not considered, and as he intended be in Ragglestone for some time sorting out Lord Prescot and his spectral rats, it would not a bad set up, and it would keep her out of my hair as long she did not want to set it up at The Old House. Anyway, if she did she wouldn't get any patients; such was their fear of entering the house.

"And where would you set it up, there are no suitable buildings?"

Roger chimed in, "The old church hall hasn't been used in years and it would make a perfectly good surgery."

"I didn't know we had a church let alone a church hall, where was that and when was it last used? George asked Roger.

"The church was burnt down a long time ago, at the time when the vicar gave up on the villagers when they refused to dispose of the TODGER, but the church hall is still there," said Eric.

"How long ago was that," George asked although deep down he was dreading the answer.

It was Eric who replied as he rubbed his chin and said, "Seventeen hundred and something."

Why was George not surprised? One day he would have to find out what the TODGER was?

It couldn't be very big as it was in a small oblong box that resembled a coffin and was kept behind the bar.

If Irene wanted to start a GP Practice then there

was nothing George could do to stop her and at least it would keep her out of his hair.

Dinner that night was the best George had eaten since moving to Ragglestone, Maude was an excellent cook and the steak and kidney pie was a joy to eat after what he had been used to lately. She had found the old cellar which still held a few bottles of wine and they were good, not that you would call vintage, but quite good. The previous tenants who had left in a hurry must have left them in their rush to get out, from what George had been told they were falling over themselves to get into the cars, it must have been an amusing sight.

The conversation turned to the haunting of Lord Prescot and his spectral rats it was Maude who opened the conversation saying, "I could go into a trance and see if I could talk to Lord Prescot direct, but there are dangers with that. I might not be able to come back, in which case I would either have to be put on a drip forever or shocked out of it, both are quite dangerous."

George didn't like the alternatives so he told her direct, "Don't do it, I won't accept the responsibility for that situation happening."

There were nods of agreement around the table.

"I think that the photographs will suffice to prove our point, and Lord Prescot can continue haunting, it won't bother us" said George. And with that we decided to call it a night and retire to our relevant rooms.

CHAPTER SIX

George was late getting up the next day and there was no sign of breakfast, Maude was usually an early riser, but as the morning wore on there was no sign of her, he was getting concerned so he sent Irene up to see if she was alright.

Irene soon returned looking very worried.

"Maude is sitting on the floor cross-legged and eyes shut, Patch is sitting in front of her and won't allow me anywhere near, I think she is in a trance and it would be dangerous to try and wake her, even if Patch would allow me to get near, and I for one don't want to attempt that, he has got some wicked looking fangs and he is quite big."

Maude was still in a trance the next day and people were still walking around her, avoiding Patch, who growled in a way that nobody had ever heard a cat growl before when anyone went near her. Everyone was getting worried; it was Lee who came up with the idea of using the camera to see if she was communicating with any spirits.

We set up the camera and sure enough there was Lord Prescot and the rats and alongside them sitting cross-legged was Maude. She was talking but we couldn't hear what she was saying, she looked directly at us and closed her eyes, Patch wandered over to us and gave a loud meow, and Maude woke up with a deep sigh.

Her first words were, "Problem solved, I will explain it after I have something to eat."

Everyone headed for the kitchen; George had no idea that toast took so long and after a cup of tea everyone sat around the table eagerly waiting on Maude's explanation.

She looked around, it was a captive audience who were all holding their collective breaths, "His Lordship was enjoying himself with one of the maids on the kitchen floor when he was bitten by a rat in a most delicate place, that was due to the maid having put some cream on it for flavour! He let out a scream, grabbed his sword and started swiping at the other rats, the maid grabbed a meat cleaver and shouted, 'hold still I will get it'. His lordship was having none of it and ran out of the door in a panic with the maid in hot pursuit, she caught up with him and had a swipe at the rat and took off his TODGER.

"The screams could be heard down in the village, Lord Prescot collapsed from shock and loss of blood and died, they buried him in the churchyard, but the maid kept his TODGER, in case there were any comebacks with the law and she had to explain what had happened. They had a small coffin made for the TODGER and intended to bury it after everything had cooled down, but somehow it never happened and the TODGER in its own little coffin ended up behind the bar of The Oak. His Lordship says he wants it buried alongside him so he can finally rest in peace. It has to be a proper funeral with a priest present, and it has to be a Ladies only funeral."

It was only then that George realised what the toast to the TODGER was.

There was silence around the table, Maude just carried on with her toast and cup of tea. It was Irene that broke the silence, "so be it, a funeral it must be, we must consult the village, they may not like the idea of losing their permanent item from behind the bar."

Mary was sent over to fetch Miriam and ask her advice on how to get a Priest and to arrange a meeting in the Oak for that night. George said he would pay for all the drinks, that should bring them all in.

Arranging the meeting in the Oak was no problem, it was getting a Priest was the problem; this is where Maude and her contacts in religious circles came in handy.

"I can get a Priest, but you will have to put up with his peculiarities, he is convinced that he is a reincarnation of one of the medieval Popes, and if he performs any religious rites he insists that he is addressed as such. He is not very popular in the orthodox church and I am not sure whether Lord Prescot would accept him. He is an ordained priest and he is very religious, but I not very sure if Father Ignatius was defrocked after his last escapade when he appeared at the Vatican and insisted that he be enthroned."

George didn't think it was good idea to ask what the outcome of that was, but on the other hand burying a centuries old TODGER might just be down his alley.

The Oak was full, everyone was there, and some of them even brought their kids. The smile on Eric's face must have been a mile wide; it was a bonanza at the till, with soft drinks for the kids. George asked Miriam if there were any problem getting them there, she just told them that she would not be chasing for rent and that did the trick.

George thought it would be good idea to let them have a few drinks first before getting down to the subject at hand, they had been told what it was about but no details, it was the ladies only funeral that would be the sticking point. He waited for the drinks to take effect before raising the subject of this unreal situation.

George stood on a table and looked around the bar, there was silence, "As you know to get Lord Prescot to rest in peace, and I think we owe him that, there are a few things that have to be done, first we have to dig up his old grave, more than likely there will be nothing there."

Eric stood up and declared. "As you know I am the unofficial undertaker, and according to information passed down from my father and his father and his father before him, Lord Prescot was buried in a lead coffin, he would more than likely be in good condition, a bit dusty, but all there and in good condition."

Everyone agreed that Lord Prescot should have his TODGER back and the all ladies funeral should go ahead.

Maude contacted Father Ignatius and he said he would be more than pleased to carry out the funeral ritual, but someone would have to come and collect him. Unfortunately he was in some sort of monastery for deluded priests, not too far away, but some responsible person would have to collect him and sign a release form, and it had to be someone with a medical qualification. That wasn't a problem – Irene.

Irene and Maude left for the monastery and were back later on the same day Father Ignatius was with them, dressed in a white robe and with a big wooden cross on a string around his neck. He held this for George to touch and then offered his hand, which George duly shook. With no idea how to address him, Maude stepped in and said, "meet Pope Gregory."

Pope Gregory looked at George and said, "I know you think I am mad, but I really am a reincarnation, some people see ghosts, are they mad? Some would say that they were and Maude has told me what the situation here is, and I and very glad of the opportunity to be of service. There are a few things I need..."

George could see complications, and just hoped it was something easy to find, but thought that with his luck it would probably be a teenage virgin, and there was no chance of that in Ragglestone, so with some trepidation he asked what the priest wanted.

"A large, good quality brandy," he replied.

That threw George, "What do you do with the brandy?" he asked, thinking that it might be some sort of weird ritual.

"Drink it of course, I haven't had decent brandy for years."

Maude burst out laughing, and so did Ignatius, this broke the ice and George finally had a feeling that things were going to be all right.

The day of the funeral dawned, the ladies were all decked out in black and Roger's wife had the coffin with the TODGER in it. The cortege started from the

Oak, all the men were in the bar with their noses pressed against the windows, George had made sure that they were well stocked with drinks before the funeral cortege set off. Father Ignatius led them off, he had brought a bishops crosier with him and to be honest he did look the part.

The men in the Oak could see that some of the ladies, and they used the term ladies loosely, were giggling, it seemed that the drinks George had put behind the bar were responsible for that.

Eric had opened the old grave and sure enough the lead coffin was there with Lord Prescot's coat of arms still visible on the lid, and Eric, with great presence of mind, had arranged a sort of rope to lower the little coffin with the TODGER into the grave,

The coffin was opened, and sure enough there he was, a mummified Lord Prescot. Father Ignatius performed some ritual in Latin and gave some sort of blessing, Maude gave George a nudge and he nearly ended up in the hole with the TODGER.

She said, "the Lord Prescot and a host of other spirits are all around and the Lord is no longer missing a certain part of his anatomy, but they are fading, I think that most of them are now finally departing.

All the ladies returned to the Oak where George had arranged a buffet, everyone's glasses were charged and Maude proposed a toast.

"To the departed."

Everybody raised their glasses and looked to the bar and with one voice shouted, "THE DEPARTED."

CHAPTER SEVEN

A month went by and Maude had departed for her London home with a large collection of photographs of the haunting.

The reincarnation of Pope Gregory was returned the same day as the funeral to the monastery for deluded priests and no one believed him when he told them what had happened, so there was nothing new there.

Irene had opened the GP's surgery in the old church hall.

Miriam with the aid of Mary and the thoughts of her delicious cooking had finally won George over and had moved into the Old House, much to the delight of the old squire, who now relished the prospect of a rich son-in-law. Well not really a son-in-law, but the ready supply of fine whisky to provide for his old age. The villagers were pleased as the old squire would not be chasing for rent too often, so all in all things had worked out fine, and The Old House had returned to being a normal country manor

The University had refused to accept the evidence of the haunting by claiming that the camera was so advanced that it could be used to manufacture the evidence; so George was back to square one.

That was until one night when everyone was tucked up in bed and a raucous laugh and girlish giggles from the kitchen woke the household. It could not be Lord Prescot, he had finally put to rest, but on the other hand Maude had said that there were few of his relatives still hanging around after the funeral. Well that was fine for George, as it was a chance to get back at the fuddy duddy's and the University who had been poo-pooing his research for years, he thought an invite for a weekend in the country would be in order, he was going to relish that sort of revenge.

THE END. "Perhaps!"